SUMMER OF SABOTAGE

BY BOB TEMPLE
ILLUSTRATED BY CYNTHIA MARTIN

Librarian Reviewer
Marci Peschke
Librarian, Dallas Independent School District
MA Education Reading Specialist, Stephen F. Austin State University
Learning Resources Endorsement, Texas Women's University

Reading Consultant
Elizabeth Stedem
Educator/Consultant, Colorado Springs, CO
MA in Elementary Education, University of Denver, CO

STONE ARCH BOOKS
www.stonearchbooks.com

Vortex Books are published by Stone Arch Books
151 Good Counsel Drive, P.O. Box 669
Mankato, Minnesota 56002
www.stonearchbooks.com

Library of Congress Cataloging-in-Publication Data
Temple, Bob.
    Summer of Sabotage / by Bob Temple; illustrated by Cynthia
Martin.
    p. cm. — (Vortex Books)
    ISBN 978-1-4342-0799-9 (library binding)
    ISBN 978-1-4342-0895-8 (pbk.)
    [1. Vacations—Fiction. 2. Mystery and detective stories.]
I. Martin, Cynthia, ill. II. Title.
PZ7.T243Su 2009
[Fic]—dc22   2008007982

Summary: When someone is causing accidents at the local waterpark,
Daniel and Aaron decide to figure out who it is.

Art Director: Heather Kindseth
Graphic Designer: Kay Fraser

Photo Credits
Capstone Publishers/Karon Dubke, all

1 2 3 4 5 6 13 12 11 10 09 08

TABLE OF CONTENTS

CHAPTER 1
THE BEST SUMMER EVER

Every morning, Daniel Thayer woke up smiling. Summer was his favorite time of the year. Three whole months with no school, no homework, and lots of awesome weather.

This summer, he'd started his own lawn mowing business to earn some extra cash. He had ten clients, so every week, he spent a day or two mowing lawns. It was pretty hard work.

It was worth it, though. All the money he made went straight to Berry Creek Waterpark.

The waterpark had opened up ten years earlier. When he was a little kid, Daniel had gone there with his parents. He'd always been jealous of the older kids, who hung out by the pool sipping soda, eating hot dogs, and having fun. To a little kid, it seemed like heaven. What could be better than being able to spend the whole day at the waterpark with lots of friends and no parents?

Finally, he had turned fourteen. This summer, his dream of spending all his time at the waterpark was coming true.

It was one of the best summers of Daniel's life. He was old enough that his parents gave him more freedom to do things on his own. He was young enough that his parents weren't making him get a real summer job. This year, mowing lawns was enough.

Daniel felt more free than he'd ever felt in his life.

That's why every morning, Daniel woke up smiling. And today, August 10, was no different.

Daniel stretched as he got out of bed. He opened the curtains and smiled again when he saw that it was a perfect, sunny day. There wasn't a cloud in the sky.

The clock on his bedside table said that it was already 11, so Daniel knew he was alone in the house. His parents would be at work. He looked through his backpack for his cell phone. The phone was dead, so he quickly hooked it up to the charger and set the phone on his desk. Then he headed downstairs.

In the kitchen, Daniel threw a couple of pieces of bread into the toaster. The newspaper was sitting on the kitchen table, so while he waited for his bread to toast, Daniel spread the paper out on the counter.

When he saw the headline on the front page, his mouth fell open.

"Another Close Call at Berry Creek," the headline read.

Daniel leaned closer to read the article. "Disaster was narrowly avoided at Berry Creek Waterpark in Durham yesterday," the article began. "Seventeen-year-old Janie Willberg was on duty at the lifeguard station Sunday near the main diving pool when 15-year-old Kyle Gage slipped on the edge of the pool. As Gage slid into the pool, he hit his head on the ground. Willberg reacted quickly, pulling Gage to safety. The incident, which is the second time this summer that the safety of Berry Creek has been called into question, has some parents in Durham worried that the waterpark isn't as safe as it has claimed."

Daniel stopped reading. "Wow," he whispered.

Kyle was always at the pool. Daniel had even talked to him a couple of times. He couldn't believe that Kyle had nearly drowned.

Daniel had forgotten about his toast, so he jumped when, suddenly, the toaster made a loud noise. Daniel stood over the sink and shoved the food into his mouth. He had planned to relax for a while that morning. *No time for that now*, he thought. *I have to get to the park!*

When he was done eating, Daniel headed upstairs. He knew his phone wouldn't be fully charged, but that didn't matter. He had to call Aaron.

Aaron was Daniel's best friend. They went to Berry Creek together every day. Aaron had to spend the mornings watching his little sister, so they usually left for the waterpark around noon.

Aaron answered on the first ring. "Did you hear about the park?" he asked.

"Yeah, I just saw the paper," Daniel answered. "It must have happened after we left yesterday."

"I can't believe it," Aaron said. "Stuff like that keeps happening at the park."

"What do you mean?" Daniel asked. "I thought this was the second accident of the summer. That doesn't seem like a big deal."

"No, it's the third one," Aaron told him. "The first one happened when a kid went down the big green slide too soon after another kid, and landed on top of him. Remember? Janie said it happened because the signal light they use wasn't working."

"I remember now," Daniel said. "The other one was when the ladder broke on the high dive. Janie was the lifeguard for all of them."

"She's really a good lifeguard," Aaron said. "I guess that's why she's getting the award."

"What award?" Daniel asked.

"Didn't you read the whole article in the paper? It said that the mayor is giving Janie a special award. There's a ceremony at the waterpark at 1," Aaron told Daniel. "I was thinking I'd go. Want to come?"

Daniel checked his watch. It wasn't even 11:30 yet. "Sure," he said. "Let me take a shower, and then I'll ride my bike over to your house and meet you."

"Sounds good," Aaron said.

Daniel shook his head as he hung up and plugged the phone back into the charger. *Why are there so many accidents happening at the waterpark?* he wondered. *Good thing Janie is there to save everybody.*

CHAPTER 2
BRAVE AND FEARLESS

After his shower, Daniel threw on a pair of swim trunks and a T-shirt. Then he sent a text message to his mom.

"Going to BC," he wrote. "Home for dinner."

Almost immediately, his phone rang. It was his mom. "Honey, are you sure you want to go to the waterpark today?" she asked. She sounded stressed.

"Yeah. Why?" Daniel asked.

His mom sighed. "After what happened yesterday, I'm not sure it's a great idea," she said. "I know you're careful, but it makes me nervous. Couldn't you and Aaron see a movie?"

"And miss out on going to the park?" Daniel asked. "There are only three weeks left of summer. I'm not wasting an entire day inside a freezing cold movie theater!"

"Daniel, I'd really feel more comfortable if you did," his mom said.

Daniel frowned. He said, "Mom, I really just want to go to the ceremony for Janie. I probably won't even get in the pool. Is it okay if I go to the ceremony and maybe stick around long enough to say hi to my friends?"

"Fine," his mom said. "Just promise me you'll be careful. It seems like a lot has been going wrong at Berry Creek, and I don't want to see anything happen to you."

Daniel rolled his eyes, but he said, "Okay, I promise, Mom."

"Okay. See you later," his mom said.

"Later!" Daniel said. He hung up. Then he stepped into his flip-flops and headed for the door. Before he left, he ran back and grabbed a beach towel. He wasn't planning to spend time in the water, but it wouldn't hurt to have his towel. *Maybe if it's really hot I can just take a quick dip*, he thought.

Daniel checked his watch. It was already 12:30. He'd have to hurry. He locked the front door behind him. Then he hopped on his bike and headed toward Aaron's house.

Aaron lived two blocks away. He only had to babysit his sister until noon every day, so Daniel knew his friend would be ready to go. He was right. Aaron came outside as soon as Daniel neared his driveway.

Traffic got heavier as they turned off Aaron's residential street onto County Road 7. Just a few minutes later, they turned onto Addison Street. About halfway down the street, there was a big iron gate that opened onto Berry Creek's parking lot.

Daniel and Aaron pedaled faster through the parking lot.

After they locked up their bikes outside the park, they flashed their season passes at the ticket booth. With the money they made from their first few weeks of lawn mowing and babysitting, Daniel and Aaron had bought season passes to the waterpark.

Hank, the guy working, smiled. "Better hurry, guys," he said. "The mayor just got here."

Aaron groaned. "Great. No lunch for me," he said.

Daniel laughed. "You'll make it," he said.

They walked to the middle of the park. A podium had been set up on a temporary stage.

Daniel squinted against the bright midday sun. "Who's that with Janie?" he asked. The tall, blond lifeguard was standing on the stage next to three other men. Daniel recognized one of them as Gabe Alexander, the waterpark's manager.

"The guy in the suit is the mayor," Aaron said. "You don't recognize the mayor?"

"It's not like he's a friend of mine or anything," Daniel said.

Gabe walked up to the microphone. "We're here to honor Janie Willberg," Gabe said. Everyone in the audience clapped and cheered. "The mayor of Durham would like to say a few words," Gabe went on.

He stepped back, and the mayor, who looked too warm in his dark blue suit, stepped forward. "Janie Willberg is an example to us all," the mayor began. "Janie's bravery as a lifeguard has been proven time and again here at Berry Creek Waterpark. She has shown herself to be the exact kind of citizen I am most proud to have in Durham. She is brave and fearless."

"Don't those words all mean the same thing?" Aaron whispered to Daniel. The man next to them shot him a dirty look.

The mayor went on, "It is my distinct honor and high privilege to present Janie Willberg with this plaque, naming her Durham's Bravest Lifeguard. You're a real hero, Janie."

Janie stepped forward, and the mayor handed her a shiny gold plaque.

Everyone clapped again. The mayor shook her hand, and then pointed at the microphone. Janie blushed, but she walked to the microphone.

The crowd grew silent. "Thank you so much," Janie said. "I'm really honored to receive this award. But I was just doing my job," she added.

"Doing it better than anyone else!" the man standing next to Daniel and Adam shouted out. "I'm her father," he told the people near him.

"That explains it," Aaron whispered.

On the stage, Janie smiled. "Thanks, Dad," she said. Laughter ran through the crowd. "And thanks, everyone," Janie added.

Everyone clapped and cheered. Then Gabe stepped back up to the microphone and said, "Okay, you can all get back in the water now."

When they heard that, all of the kids in the park cheered even louder. Daniel glanced at Janie. She frowned. But then she looked down at the plaque in her hands and smiled.

"Let's go talk to her," Aaron said. He and Daniel pushed through the crowd toward Janie.

This was Janie's first year as a lifeguard, but she'd been a regular at the waterpark for as long as they could remember. As soon as Janie had become a lifeguard, Daniel had noticed that she'd changed a little. She was focused on her job. She was always the first one to jump in the water at the smallest sign of danger. One time, she even jumped in to save Daniel when he wasn't in trouble at all. He was only doing the dead-man's float.

As they struggled to get through the crowd, Daniel felt a hand on his shoulder. He turned and saw Gabe.

"Hey, Gabe," Daniel said. "Pretty cool about Janie."

"Yeah, I hope it's enough to save us," Gabe muttered.

"What do you mean?" Aaron asked. "Save us from what?"

"Oh, never mind," Gabe said, shaking his head. "Listen, guys, I have to talk to you. Can you come into the office with me, please?"

"Can we say hi to Janie first?" Aaron asked. "I don't want to be the last guy to congratulate her."

Gabe frowned. "I'm sorry, but this can't wait," he said. "We have a problem."

"What kind of problem?" Daniel asked. He looked at Aaron, who shrugged.

"My office. Now," Gabe said.

CHAPTER 3
A WEEK?

Daniel and Aaron were used to Gabe being worried about something. He was a nice guy, but he always walked around with a frown on his face.

He worried about kids getting hurt. He worried about food safety at the hot dog stand. He worried when the park wasn't busy enough, and he worried when it was too crowded.

Gabe was always worried about something. But he almost never got mad.

Today, as Daniel and Aaron followed Gabe to his office, they were sure of one thing: Gabe was really angry. He'd never called them into his office before.

Daniel and Aaron had to hurry to keep up with Gabe. "What did we do?" Aaron whispered.

"I have no clue," Daniel whispered back. "But whatever it was, it wasn't good."

Inside the office building, the two boys followed Gabe down a long hallway that had doors on both sides. Their flip-flops made slapping noises on the slippery concrete floor. Gabe stopped in front of one door and opened it. Daniel and Aaron walked inside.

Gabe's office contained a desk, a bookshelf, and two chairs for visitors. Books and papers were stacked on every flat surface. A plant with dry, brown leaves sat on the windowsill.

The window was open, and through it, Daniel could hear the noise of kids in the park, shrieking as they went down slides and laughing and talking as they hung out next to the pool.

"What's going on?" Aaron asked as Gabe walked into the room and shut the office door. "We haven't gotten in the water yet. We want to get going before the lines get too long."

Gabe frowned. "You may not be getting in the water at all today, I'm afraid," he said.

"What are you talking about?" Daniel said. "We can't be in trouble. We just got here."

Gabe sat down behind his desk. He motioned for the boys to sit down. They glanced at each other, and then slowly sat down.

"This isn't about today," Gabe said. He leaned forward.

"This is about yesterday," Gabe went on. "Let me ask you a question. When you leave here, how do you go home?"

Daniel looked over at Aaron. "We get on Addison Street and take it straight to County Road 7. Why?" Daniel asked.

"I should be more specific," Gabe said, shaking his head. "How do you get from the waterpark to Addison Street?"

"Usually, we go to the end of the parking lot and take a right," Aaron told him. "But sometimes, we cut through the back yards."

Aaron told Gabe that the day before, he and Daniel had been hanging out by the pool when they realized that Aaron was going to be late for dinner. They'd taken off in a hurry. Since they didn't have much time, they'd taken a shortcut through a couple of the back yards that were near the waterpark.

As they hurried through the yards, Aaron had sped past Daniel. He was going too fast, though, and he accidentally cut Daniel off with his back tire. That sent Daniel flying into a flowerbed in one of the yards. He'd messed up the flowers pretty badly. And since they were so late, instead of telling the person who lived in the house, they'd just taken off.

"Seriously, though, Gabe," Daniel said after Aaron finished telling the story, "we were going to go back and apologize today. As soon as we left the park."

Gabe sighed. "Well, I'm sorry, but that's too little too late," he said. "Do you have any idea how big a deal this is? Do you have any idea whose house that was? Do you know whose petunias you rode your bikes through?"

"We didn't ride our bikes through the flowers," Aaron muttered. "Daniel just fell into them."

"This is no time for jokes," Gabe said. "Those flowers belong to a woman named Lucy Parker."

"Who's that?" Daniel asked.

"You are unbelievable," Gabe said. He sat back in his chair and put his hands over his eyes. Daniel could hear the sounds of happy, laughing kids through the window. He looked over at Aaron. His friend was frowning down at his shoes. When he'd gotten up that morning, Daniel never expected his day to turn so bad so fast.

Finally, Gabe looked at them. He spoke clearly, quietly, and slowly, but Daniel could tell that the park manager was really upset.

"Lucy Parker," Gabe began, "is the reason that Berry Creek Waterpark exists. And now she wishes it didn't."

CHAPTER 4
LUCY PARKER'S PETUNIAS

Aaron and Daniel looked at each other, shocked. Why would someone wish that the waterpark didn't exist? What kind of person was Lucy Parker?

As if he'd read their minds, Gabe said, "Lucy Parker isn't the kind of person you want mad at you."

"Does she own the park?" Daniel asked.

"No," Gabe answered. "The city owns the land the park is built on."

"So what does Lucy Parker have to do with Berry Creek?" Aaron asked.

Gabe fiddled with some pieces of paper on his desk. "Well," he began, "the city didn't always own the land."

It turned out that the land that Berry Creek was built on had once been part of a huge estate. It was owned by a rich couple.

As the couple got older, they realized that they didn't need so much land. They began giving chunks of their estate to the city. When they donated the land, the couple would tell the city how they wanted that piece of land to be used.

One plot of land was used to build the senior center. Another was used to build an addition to the hospital. Another plot was used to build a new City Hall building. An office building was built on another part.

"The piece of land we're on now was donated about fifteen years ago," Gabe said. "The husband had just died, and the wife donated their last remaining piece of property. She told the city that she wanted the land to be kept wild and turned into a walking path for people like her, who enjoyed flowers and plants and being outside."

"So why did they turn it into a waterpark?" Daniel asked.

"Well, you guys wouldn't remember this, because you were really little," Gabe told them. "But fifteen years ago, this city wasn't great for kids. There weren't many places that they could go to play safely. That's all changed now, and this waterpark is a big part of why that happened."

"I get it," Aaron said slowly. "The city needed a place for kids more than they needed flowers."

"Right," Gabe said. "But there were two big problems with that. The woman didn't like children, and the land she had donated was located right behind her home."

Daniel said nervously, "The woman who donated the land was Lucy Parker, right?"

"That's right," Gabe said. "Ever since we opened this park, she's been complaining to the police about the kids, the noise, everything. She wants nothing more than to see us shut down. And now, you two have wrecked her flowers."

Daniel and Aaron looked guiltily at each other. "We'll plant new flowers," Aaron said.

"We'll go apologize," Daniel said.

"Don't bother," Gabe said. "She called the police. They told me I need to take action."

"What kind of action?" Daniel asked.

Gabe shrugged. "I have to do something," he said. "If I get too many complaints, the police can close us down. That's exactly what Lucy Parker wants. And we're already in trouble because of all of the accidents that have been happening around here."

"How can you be in trouble?" Aaron asked. "They just gave Janie an award!"

"Yes, Janie got an award for being the one who made those rescues, but I'm in trouble because the accidents happened in the first place," Gabe said. "The city wanted a safe place for kids, remember? Not someplace parents are afraid to let their kids go."

"It's a waterpark," Aaron said. "There are always going to be accidents."

"I don't know," Gabe muttered. "These don't really feel like accidents."

"What do you mean?" Daniel asked.

But Gabe waved his hand. "Never mind," he said. "Anyway, I have to do something, so I can tell the police that I've done something. Then they can tell Mrs. Parker that we punished you. I've thought about it, and . . ."

"Oh no," Aaron whispered.

Gabe managed a small smile. "It's not the end of the world," he said. "I'm just going to take away your season passes for one week."

Aaron's jaw dropped, and Daniel felt his face turn really hot. "A whole week?" he whispered. "There are only three weeks left of summer!"

"Sorry, guys," Gabe said. "Be more careful around Lucy Parker's petunias next time."

He stood up and held out his hand. Aaron and Daniel dug into their pockets. They put their season passes in Gabe's hand. Then they walked out the door.

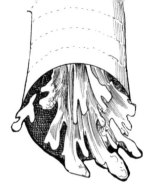

CHAPTER 5
ON PURPOSE?

The week that Daniel and Aaron spent without their Berry Creek season passes was the longest week of their lives.

At first, Daniel didn't have trouble keeping busy. He added a couple of lawn mowing clients. The first few days, he mowed lawns for eight hours straight. Afterward, he just headed home, had dinner, and went straight to bed.

On Saturday morning, Daniel woke up smiling, as usual.

Then, when he rolled over and glanced at his clock, he suddenly remembered. He couldn't go to the waterpark that day. Then he stared at the ceiling. *Great*, he thought. *What am I supposed to do today?*

Every Saturday morning for the last nine weeks, he and Aaron had headed straight to the waterpark. Aaron didn't have to watch his sister on the weekend, which meant they got in at least a few extra hours on the slides and in the pool. There hadn't been one Saturday when it rained, or was too cold, or that they hadn't been able to go. Today would've been another perfect day.

Daniel groaned. The day wouldn't be perfect anymore. In fact, it could be the worst day of the summer.

Just as he was about to try to fall back asleep, to waste a few more hours, his phone rang.

Daniel got out of bed and dug through his backpack. He found the phone wedged into the front pocket. It was Aaron. He quickly flipped it open.

"What are we going to do today?" Aaron said. "I can't believe how nice it is outside. I don't have to watch Claire, you don't have to mow lawns, and we can't go to the waterpark. This is the worst day of my life."

Daniel laughed bitterly. "I know," he said. "Do you want to ride our bikes to the mall?"

"The mall?" Aaron asked. "No way. The mall is inside. I want to be outside!"

"What about the beach?" Daniel suggested. "It's not the same, but it would take us a while to get there on our bikes, so that would kill some time. And there's a hot dog stand there."

"No cotton candy, though," Aaron said sadly.

"Right," Daniel said. "No cotton candy."

Aaron was quiet for a few seconds. Finally, he sighed loudly. "Fine," he said. "Let's go to the boring beach."

* * *

Half an hour later, Daniel pedaled up Aaron's driveway. Aaron was sitting on the front steps of his house, looking angry.

"What's wrong?" Daniel asked, hopping off his bike and sitting down next to Aaron.

"Nothing," Aaron said. "I'm just mad that we can't go to Berry Creek. The hot dogs at the beach aren't nearly as good as the waterpark hot dogs."

"They're from the same company," Daniel said.

"Who cares?" Aaron said. "They don't taste as good!"

Daniel decided to change the subject. All week, he hadn't been able to stop thinking about something Gabe had said.

"Aaron, did you think Gabe was acting weird the day he took our passes away?" he asked. "He seemed really upset."

"Well, yeah," Aaron said. "We wrecked Mrs. Parker's petunias."

"I know, but he seemed more upset than that," Daniel went on. "And remember, he said he didn't think the accidents were accidents?"

"What do you think he meant?" Aaron asked.

"I think he's trying to say that someone is making these things happen on purpose," Daniel said.

Both of them were quiet for a few minutes.

Finally, Daniel said, "The kid who got hurt at the waterpark on Monday slipped on the deck next to the pool, right? He fell, hit his head, and fell into the water. And that's when Janie jumped in to save him."

"Right," Aaron said.

"How could that be on purpose?" Daniel asked.

Aaron shrugged. "It couldn't," he said. "Pool decks are slippery. Kids fall all the time. I think Gabe is worried about nothing."

"What if someone did something to make that pool deck more slippery than usual?" Daniel asked.

"That's crazy," Aaron said. "Who would want to hurt a bunch of kids at the waterpark?"

"Gabe said Mrs. Parker didn't like kids," Daniel reminded him.

Aaron rolled his eyes. "That doesn't mean she wants to kill them," he said.

Daniel laughed. "Yeah, you're right," he said. "What about the other accidents? Could someone have made them happen?"

"No way," Aaron said. "The first one happened because the signal light broke. I think the light bulb was old or something."

Daniel shook his head. "That's a weird one, but I don't know how someone could do that on purpose," he said.

"The other one was when the ladder broke on the high dive," Aaron said. "One of the steps in the ladder just snapped in half."

"Hmm," Daniel said. "That one is a little fishy."

"I guess it is," Aaron said. "But I still think this is crazy. Why would anyone want to cause accidents at the waterpark?"

Daniel looked at Aaron and raised his eyebrows. "Well, we know that Lucy Parker wants the waterpark to close," Daniel said. "Gabe said if he had too many accidents and complaints, the park might have to close."

Aaron started laughing.

"What's so funny?" Daniel asked.

"You are!" Aaron said, still laughing. "You're trying to tell me that some old lady, who likes going for walks and planting petunias, has been sneaking into the park and trying to make kids break their legs so that she can have her walking path back? You're nuts!"

"Okay, maybe it's crazy," Daniel admitted. "But something weird is going on over there."

Aaron stood up and started walking to his bike. "I'm starving," he said. "Let's go get some hot dogs."

CHAPTER 6
THEY'LL DO ANYTHING

The beach was deserted when they rode their bikes up. Even the hot dog stand was boarded up and closed.

"This is awful!" Aaron said. "Everybody in the whole city except for us is at the waterpark!"

"Us and Mrs. Parker," Daniel joked.

Aaron made a face. "She's probably there too, going down the waterslide right now!" he yelled.

Daniel laughed. "We might as well head home," he said. "My mom will make us something to eat, if you're hungry."

"You know I am," Aaron grumbled.

The boys hopped back on their bikes and rode home. Daniel's mom was outside working in her garden when they rode up the driveway. She pushed the hair out of her face and smiled. "You boys are home early," she said. "Is the park too crowded?"

Daniel frowned. "Mom, I told you that we can't go there this week," he said.

"That's right," his mom said. "Aaron's mom and I were talking, and we think that you should offer to help Mrs. Parker with some lawn work," she added.

"She doesn't like kids," Daniel mumbled.

"Come on," his mom said. "I'll make you guys some lunch."

They followed her into the house and sat at the kitchen table while she made a stack of turkey sandwiches.

"I'm sorry that you can't go to the waterpark on a day like this," Daniel's mom said. "But it's probably better that you stay away from the waterpark for a while anyway. There's some strange stuff going on there."

"You mean the accidents?" Daniel said.

"Yes and no," Daniel's mom said. "There's more going on there than you probably know about."

"You always know everything that's going on, Mrs. Thayer," Aaron said.

"That's because I'm on the city council," she told him. "And at last month's city council meeting, there was a lot of talk about Berry Creek Waterpark."

"What do you mean?" Daniel asked.

His mom set the plate of sandwiches on the table. Daniel and Aaron each grabbed one.

"Are you sure you want to hear a bunch of boring city council stuff?" Daniel's mom asked.

Daniel and Aaron looked at each other. "Yeah," Daniel said. "I think it's interesting."

Daniel's mom shrugged. "Okay," she said. "Well, at last month's meeting, a man from GigaMart came to talk to us. He's been trying to get a GigaMart built here in town for a few months now, but we've turned him down every time."

"Why?" Aaron asked. "It would be awesome if we had a GigaMart here."

Daniel's mom laughed. "Well, he had a specific place in mind," she said. "But the location isn't set up to have a huge building built on it."

She reached over and grabbed a sandwich. She took a few bites before she went on. "Now he's trying to buy the land that the waterpark is located on, so he can build the GigaMart there," she said. "But the city council wants to keep it as a waterpark. Anyway, the man was really mad when we voted to not let him buy the land."

"Another one," Daniel muttered, looking at Aaron.

"What?" his mom said. "Another what?"

"Oh, nothing," Daniel said. His mom frowned, and Daniel could tell that she was going to ask him what was going on. But just then, the telephone rang in the other room. His mom went to answer it.

Daniel and Aaron each grabbed another sandwich, and without speaking, they headed upstairs to Daniel's room.

"So, that's another person who would be happy if there were accidents happening at the park," Daniel said once they were upstairs. "If the park had to close, that GigaMart guy would be able to buy the land. And he would probably be able to buy it cheap."

"I still think you're wrong," Aaron said. "Someone could've gotten really hurt in those accidents at the park. Maybe even killed! The guy who hit his head and fell into the water was knocked out. He would have drowned if Janie hadn't jumped in. Do you think Lucy Parker or the guy from GigaMart would be willing to kill someone just to get what they want?"

"I don't know," Daniel said. "But my mom has talked about people like that before. Some of them will do anything to get their building built."

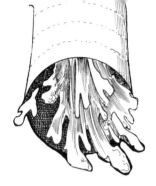

CHAPTER 7
BACK TO BERRY CREEK

Three days, dozens of sandwiches, and a lot of lawn mowing later, it was time for Daniel and Aaron to return to the waterpark. Daniel woke up earlier than normal on Tuesday morning and rode his bike to Aaron's. He planned to hang out there until Aaron was done babysitting. Then they'd ride over to Berry Creek together.

Aaron opened the door as soon as Daniel got there. "Great news," Aaron said. "My sister has a cold!"

Daniel frowned. "It's kind of mean to be glad that your sister is sick," he said.

"I'm not glad she's sick," Aaron said. "I'm glad that it means my mom stayed home from work. That means I don't have to babysit. And that, my friend, means we can leave right now!"

Gabe was standing by the entrance gate when Daniel and Aaron locked up their bikes outside the waterpark. He walked over to them, and Daniel could see that he was holding their season passes.

"Welcome back, boys," Gabe said, smiling. "It's nice to see you again. How did your week go with no waterpark?"

"Not good," Aaron said. "I think Daniel's cracking up."

Gabe laughed. "What's the trouble, Daniel?" he asked.

"I can't stop thinking about what you said to us about the accidents," Daniel said. "That maybe they weren't really accidents at all."

Gabe chuckled and shook his head. "Oh, I'm sorry if I made you guys worry," he said. "I was just really stressed out that day from everything that was going on. There's no big conspiracy here. We just had some bad luck."

Gabe handed them their passes. "Welcome back to Berry Creek," he said. Then he turned and started walking away.

"Hey Gabe, wait a second," Daniel called after him.

Gabe turned. "I've got to get back to work," he said.

"I know," Daniel said. "But I think we can help. I know Mrs. Parker wants the park closed. I think I know some other people who do too. Those weren't accidents!"

Gabe shook his head, smiling. "Daniel, you have a really big imagination," he said. "Those were all accidents, and that's all there is to it."

"That's what I've been telling him!" Aaron said. "Come on, Daniel, let's hit the slides!"

Daniel sighed. "Fine," he said. "Let's go."

The boys headed to the locker room, where they threw their passes and towels into gray metal lockers. Then they headed out to the big green slide.

Once they'd gone down the slide, they hurried back in line to do it again. Then they headed over to the wave pool. After that, they stopped at the diving pool to take a few leaps off the high dive.

The weather was perfect. It was sunny and warm. The park was packed with kids. Everyone was having a great time.

Daniel was having so much fun that he forgot all about the weird accidents in the park.

Finally, after about five hours, both Daniel and Aaron needed a break. They each bought a couple of hot dogs. Daniel got a chocolate shake, too. Then they grabbed their towels and lay down on beach chairs next to the diving pool.

They were quiet, just eating their food and enjoying the warm sunshine.

Aaron squinted as he looked over at the diving board. "Whoa," he said. "Connor's getting ready to jump."

Daniel looked over too. "He has some serious skills," he said. "By the time he's in high school, he's going to be amazing."

"He could be in the Olympics," Aaron said. "He's next, after this kid."

The boy in front of Connor did an easy jump off the board. Daniel narrowed his eyes. *Is the board wobbling?* he wondered.

As the kid dove down toward the water, Daniel jumped up from his chair.

"Did you see that?" Daniel shouted. "There's something wrong with that board! Look at it wobble!"

"It's a diving board," Aaron said, rolling his eyes. "They all wobble."

Connor walked to the end of the board. He reached the tip and leaped into the air. The board wobbled, but it wasn't the right kind of wobble. A diving board should bounce. This one looked like it was going to break.

Aaron gasped. "You're right, something's wrong," he said. And as Connor landed on the end of the diving board, the board broke in half.

Connor fell toward the water, screaming.

Everyone in the diving area froze. Daniel stared, mouth open, as the diving board hit the water.

As the board smashed flat on the surface of the water, it made a loud *slap*! Everyone watching gasped. Then Connor hit the water. His left side smacked into the board.

In an instant, Janie dove into the water. It seemed like she was in the water before Connor was.

Janie quickly pulled Connor out of the pool as Daniel, Aaron, and a hundred other kids looked on.

"Move out of the way!" someone yelled. Daniel spun around. Gabe was running toward the diving pool. Everyone moved so that he could get through to Connor and Janie.

"Is he breathing?" Gabe asked Janie.

"Yes. He's breathing and he's awake. But I think his shoulder is out of joint. Are you in pain, Connor?" Janie asked.

Connor moaned. "My arm hurts really bad," he said.

"We need to get him to the hospital right away," Gabe said. "I'll stay with him. Go call an ambulance."

Janie got up and started running toward the office building.

Daniel looked at Aaron. "Do you still think these are all accidents?" Daniel asked.

"No," Aaron whispered. "No, I don't."

CHAPTER 8
THE TRUTH IS BAD ENOUGH

Daniel rushed over to Gabe, who was sitting on the edge of the pool and talking to Connor. All the other kids were still standing around. Some of them were on cell phones, telling other people about what had happened. No one dared get near the pool.

"Not now, Daniel," Gabe muttered when he saw Daniel. "I don't have time to talk. This is an emergency." He stood up and walked toward his office.

"Okay, fine," Daniel said.

As Daniel walked back over toward Aaron, he heard a younger kid telling a group of boys that he had seen someone loosening the bolts on the diving board.

Daniel stopped and grabbed the kid's sleeve. "Don't make it worse than it really is," he snapped. "The truth is bad enough."

The younger boy looked scared. "Sorry," he said quietly.

A woman wearing a skirt and high heels ran up to the pool. She had a camera around her neck.

"She must be a reporter," Aaron said.

He and Daniel watched the woman snap photos of Connor. The woman walked to the pool and started taking pictures of the broken diving board. It was still floating in the water.

Then she started talking to kids who were standing around near the pool.

The reporter walked over to Daniel and asked, "Were you nearby when the tragedy happened?"

Daniel rolled his eyes. "No, I wasn't," he said. "We were on the other side of the park."

The reporter walked away, and Aaron turned to Daniel. "Why did you say that?" he asked. "We could've been in the paper!"

Daniel shook his head. "That would've made it worse," he explained. "Let's just say for one second that I'm right and someone is trying to shut down the park. If there's more bad stuff in the paper, then that person is getting exactly what they want!"

"Fine," Aaron mumbled. "It still would've been cool to be in the paper, though."

All around them, kids stood in small groups, talking and whispering. Some parents had started arriving to pick up their kids.

No one had been allowed to get back into the water, so the hot dog stand had a line that reached for what seemed like miles.

Frowning, Gabe walked back toward the diving pool. Everyone got quiet as he approached. "I need your attention," Gabe yelled. "Sorry, kids, but we're closing down for the rest of the day. You'll have to get your stuff and go."

"Will Berry Creek be open tomorrow?" a girl asked.

Gabe sighed. "I don't know," he said.

CHAPTER 9
LIFEGUARD OF THE YEAR

Daniel and Aaron found themselves walking next to Janie as they headed to the locker building.

"Hey, Janie," Daniel said. "Another great save."

Janie looked over and smiled. "Thanks," she said.

"You were amazing!" Aaron said. He blushed. "It was almost like you were in the water before he even hit."

The smile faded from Janie's face. "Yeah, well, I saw the board come loose on his first bounce, so I knew it was going to be bad," she replied. "Instead of waiting for him to fall, I just reacted and got in the water right away."

"Don't you think it's a little too much of a coincidence, all these accidents happening?" Daniel said. "I mean, do you think they're really accidents?"

They walked to the entrance of the locker building. Janie pulled the door open, and the three of them entered the air-conditioned lobby area.

"I haven't thought about it like that," she said. She stopped outside the girls' locker room and turned to face Aaron and Daniel. "I was too busy making the rescues to think much about why they were happening. I guess it is a little strange."

"Have you noticed anything else that was weird?" Daniel asked.

Aaron laughed. "Don't mind my friend," he told Janie. "He thinks everything is an evil plot."

Janie smiled. "It's okay. No, I haven't seen anything weird," she told Daniel. Then she frowned. "Well, now that you mention it," she went on, "there was something that I thought was pretty weird today."

Daniel leaned closer. "What?" he asked. "What did you see? You can tell me whatever it was," he added.

Janie laughed. "I saw a kid with crazy ideas," she said, winking at Daniel. "Nothing weird is going on. Come on, seriously. There have been more accidents than normal, but luckily, I've been around to help the kids who got hurt. That's all that's happening."

She looked over at the Wall of Honor, across the hall from the locker rooms. The brick wall was covered with pictures of lifeguards, famous people at the park, events, and parties. There were also some awards that the park and its employees had won. Those plaques looked a lot like the one that Janie had gotten from the mayor, which also hung on the wall.

Janie stepped toward the wall to get a closer look. "Unbelievable," she said, shaking her head. "All those rescues, and they put my plaque down there."

She pointed to a spot in the middle of the wall where her plaque had been mounted. "Mine belongs up here, way above her picture," Janie said. She pointed at a picture right above her plaque. There was a sign next to the picture that read, "Lifeguard of the Year, 2007."

"I remember her," Aaron said, pointing at the picture. "She was a great lifeguard. Everybody always said she was the best lifeguard Berry Creek ever had."

"Yeah, I know," Janie said loudly. She took a deep breath and added, "That's Grace. She's my older sister." She shook her head. Then she turned and headed into the girls' locker room.

Daniel watched the door swing shut. Then he leaned closer to Aaron and whispered, "I think we have another suspect."

Aaron nodded slowly. "This is getting too strange," he said.

After they emptied their lockers, Aaron and Daniel headed out of the park. Gabe was standing near the entrance gate.

As Daniel got closer, he could hear that Gabe was apologizing to each person who left the park.

"I'm so sorry about this," Gabe was saying. "This isn't what you expect from Berry Creek, and we're going to figure out what went wrong." He kept repeating how sorry he was. Then he yelled, "Don't worry! The park will reopen tomorrow!"

Daniel and Aaron stopped in front of Gabe. "Still think this is all just bad luck?" Daniel asked.

Gabe frowned. "Yes, Daniel, I do," he said sternly. "You need to put this conspiracy stuff out of your mind. When I said I didn't know if they were accidents, I was angry and upset. I wasn't thinking."

He shook his head. Then he went on, "Maybe you should take another day or two off from the waterpark. Get your minds off of all this and think about something else."

"Maybe," Daniel said slowly.

Then he and Aaron left. They quickly unlocked their bikes and started riding out of the parking lot.

"Hold on a second," Aaron said. "Do you see that?"

Daniel turned. Aaron was pointing toward the back yards they used for shortcuts. There, sitting on the deck behind her house, was Lucy Parker. She was peering at the waterpark through a pair of binoculars.

"Whoa," Daniel whispered. "She's spying on the waterpark!"

"She totally is," Aaron said.

"Do you think she hired someone to break the diving board today?" Daniel asked, getting excited. "And now she's making sure that the job was done?"

"I don't know," Aaron said. "But I am starting to believe your crazy ideas."

CHAPTER 10
FOLLOW THE MONEY

They went to Daniel's house to eat some sandwiches. "Let's start with what we know," Daniel said.

"We know that the accidents at the park are being caused by someone," Aaron said.

"Sort of," Daniel said. "That's what we're trying to prove. We don't know it for a fact."

"Okay," Aaron said. "Then we know for a fact that Mrs. Parker doesn't like kids. And we know that she didn't want her land used the way it was. She wanted a walking path."

Daniel nodded. "We know that she watches the waterpark," he said. "And we know that there's a guy from GigaMart who's not happy that the city didn't sell him the land."

"Don't forget about Janie," Aaron said.

"How could I, after what she said today?" Daniel said. "She's jealous of her sister. And she's really proud of herself for these rescues."

"What about Gabe?" Aaron added. "He's acting weird too."

"Yeah," Daniel said. "At first he said these weren't accidents. But then he said they were, and that it wasn't a big deal. And he doesn't want us around looking at stuff."

"Do you really think any of these people are behind the accidents?" Aaron asked.

"They all have motives," Daniel said. "There are reasons that each of them would be happy there were accidents at the park."

"I know Gabe's been acting weird, but I can't think of a motive for him," Aaron said. "Why would he want the park closed?"

"Wait a minute," Daniel said. "When my mom talks about city council stuff, she always says that when there's something weird going on, you should follow the money."

"What does that mean?" Aaron asked.

"It means that money is a motive for a lot of things," Daniel said. "So Gabe's motive could be that someone is paying him. What if someone is giving Gabe money to create the accidents? That would be a motive for him to do it, right?"

Daniel smacked himself in the forehead. "I can't believe I didn't think of this earlier!" he yelled. "To shut down the waterpark, they need people to know about the accidents. I bet Gabe called the reporter, too."

(77)

"That's crazy," Aaron said. "I don't know who called the reporter, but it just doesn't make sense for it to be Janie or Gabe. If the waterpark closes, they're out of a job!"

Daniel stood up. "Well, one thing's for sure," he said. "Whoever is doing this is doing it when no one is in the park. Like right now. I say we head back over there."

Aaron sighed, but he stood up too. "The only reason I'm coming," he told Daniel, "is because I think you've gone crazy, and I can't let a crazy person go off on his own."

"Whatever works," Daniel said.

CHAPTER 11
GIGAMART WORLDWIDE, INC.

When they were close enough to see the waterpark, Daniel and Aaron locked up their bikes in the woods. Then they crept up to the fence at the back of the waterpark.

"Shhh!" Daniel said suddenly. "There's a guy working on the diving board." The man was on a big lift, up near the top of the diving board.

"Look over there," Aaron said, pointing toward the biggest waterslide in the park. "There's another guy working on that slide."

"We need to see where these guys are from," Daniel said.

"Well, that's easy," Aaron said. "We just have to see what their truck says. It's over there."

Crouching, Aaron and Daniel moved slowly toward the front of the waterpark. Once they reached the side of the main building, they stood up. They scooted along the building until they reached the front corner.

Daniel peered around the corner. He got a clear view of the side of the truck.

There was a small logo on the door of the truck, along with the words "GigaMart Maintenance." But the side of the truck was painted with a huge logo and the words "GigaMart Worldwide, Inc."

Daniel and Aaron stepped back around the corner of the building and faced each other.

(81)

"Do you know what this means?" Daniel said. Before Aaron even had a chance to answer, Daniel said, "The company that is doing the repair work at the waterpark is owned by the same company that wants to build a GigaMart on this land."

"So what?" Aaron asked. "That doesn't mean anything."

"It makes them the most likely suspect," Daniel said. "If GigaMart owns the repair company, they can be ordering workers to cause the accidents at the park."

"How can we prove it?" Aaron asked.

Daniel said, "We'll need some proof, so we can get someone to believe us."

He held up his cell phone. Aaron raised an eyebrow.

"Thank goodness they put cameras in these things," Daniel said, smiling.

Daniel took a couple of pictures of the truck. "I don't know if these pictures are going to be clear enough for them to help us much," he said. He showed his pictures to Aaron on the small screen of the phone.

"Well, it's better than nothing," Aaron said.

"Let's get out of here," Daniel said. "I think we have enough evidence."

They headed away from the park. Then Aaron stopped and nudged Daniel. "Look!" Aaron said, pointing. "She's at it again!"

Daniel looked. He could see Lucy Parker sitting on her deck. She was staring through her binoculars again. This time, they were pointed right at him.

"I think she's looking at us," Aaron said.

Lucy Parker lowered her binoculars. She pointed right at the boys with her right arm. Then, she waved for the boys to come to her.

"No way," Daniel said.

"Let's get out of here," Aaron said.

"We can't do that," Daniel said. "She knows it's us. If we run, she'll just complain again, and then we'll lose our season passes for the rest of the summer. And if that happens, this mystery never gets solved."

He slowly started walking toward Mrs. Parker's yard. Aaron sighed, but he followed. When Lucy Parker saw them coming, she walked toward the fence to meet them.

Daniel was scared to even look her in the eye.

When they stood by the back fence of Mrs. Parker's yard, she spoke first. "You're the boys who ruined my flowers," she said.

But she didn't look angry. In fact, Lucy Parker was smiling.

CHAPTER 12
THE KIND OF PERSON YOU TRUST?

Mrs. Parker looked more like a kind grandmother than an angry woman who didn't like kids. "What are you doing sneaking around today?" she asked. "There aren't any flowers to wreck out there."

She was still smiling, so Daniel knew she was joking. He laughed nervously. Aaron did too.

"Boys, you can relax," Mrs. Parker said. "I'm not a mean old lady."

"That's not what we heard," Aaron said. Daniel glared at him, but Mrs. Parker laughed.

"I know, I know," she said. "A lot of people think I'm mean. But all I'm doing is trying to make sure my land is used the way I want it to be used."

"You mean the land that used to be yours, right?" Aaron asked. "The land that's now our waterpark."

"You're right," Mrs. Parker said. "I don't really own it now. The city does. But in my heart, it's still my land. All of this land around here belonged to my husband and me. He passed away a few years ago, and even though I don't own it anymore, I still look after it."

Daniel frowned. *What does she mean?* he wondered.

"I'm very concerned by all the accidents," Mrs. Parker went on. "You see, I love children, and I don't want to see anything bad happen at the waterpark."

"Wait a second," Aaron said. "You hate kids. That's why you called the cops when we wrecked your petunias."

"We're really sorry, by the way, and we'll come over and help you with yard work whenever you want," Daniel quickly added.

Mrs. Parker looked confused. "I'm not sure I understand," she said. "I didn't call the police when you boys wrecked my flowers. In fact, I've never called the police in my life!"

Aaron's mouth dropped open. "But Gabe told us!" he said.

Mrs. Parker shrugged. "Well, is Gabe the kind of person you trust?" she asked. "Or is he the kind of person you don't trust?"

Daniel shook his head. "I always thought he was the kind of person I could trust," he said quietly. "But now, I'm not so sure."

Mrs. Parker asked, "Did you get a close look at the trucks when you were over at the waterpark?"

"Yeah," Aaron told her. "They belong to GigaMart. You probably haven't heard of it, but . . ."

Mrs. Parker interrupted him. "I may be old, but I'm not that old!" she said. "Of course I have heard of GigaMart. In fact, when I gave the city the land to build the waterpark, GigaMart called me and asked me to sell the land to them instead."

"Why didn't you sell it?" Aaron asked.

"Well, unlike what your friend may have Gabe told you, I wanted to give the land to kids," Mrs. Parker told him.

"I don't think we should call Gabe our friend," Daniel said. "This is starting to all make sense."

"Sounds like the GigaMart people have gotten to him," Mrs. Parker said. "If I had to guess, I'd say they're working together to cause these accidents."

"I still find it hard to believe that Gabe would do that," Daniel said. "But I don't have any other explanation."

The sun was getting lower in the sky. "We better go," Aaron said. "I think it's almost dinner time."

"Will you let me know if you find out any information?" Mrs. Parker asked.

"Of course," Daniel said. "Now that we know you don't hate kids, we won't be so scared to be near your house!"

"Just be careful," Mrs. Parker warned them.

CHAPTER 13
"THAT'S MY SPOT!"

The next day, Daniel and Aaron nervously rode their bikes to the waterpark. They planned to avoid Gabe as much as possible. After all, if Mrs. Parker was right and Gabe was involved in the accidents, it could be dangerous to be near him.

The park was less crowded than normal, and Daniel and Aaron didn't see Gabe for the first few hours. Daniel was starting to feel more relaxed. *Maybe Gabe's not behind this after all*, he thought.

At noon, he and Aaron grabbed hot dogs and sodas at the snack stand. Then they headed to the beach chairs near the diving pool. Suddenly, Gabe popped out from behind a corner.

"Hello there," he said. "I see you didn't take my advice to stay away for a few days."

"Oh, right," Daniel said, trying to act normal. "We like it here too much."

He and Aaron sat down on a couple of beach chairs. But as Daniel was slurping up the last of his soda, he heard someone yell.

It was Janie. She screamed, "That's my spot today! You work by the high dive."

Daniel turned and saw that Janie was yelling at another lifeguard. She pushed the guy out of the way and sat down in the big wooden lifeguard chair near the giant green slide.

"Let's head over there after we eat," he whispered to Aaron.

One after another, kids flew through the twists and turns of the super-fast slide. Their screams and laughter echoed in the air.

Finally, Daniel and Aaron finished eating and got in line for the giant slide. When it was Daniel's turn, he stood on the platform at the top of the slide. Aaron was waiting right behind him.

Daniel waited for the signal light to turn green. When it did, the lifeguard at the top of the slide motioned for him to go.

Daniel dove headfirst into the tunnel. He rocketed left and right as he slid through the slide.

When he reached his favorite part, the crazy turns near the exit for the slide, he screamed with excitement.

But as he was about to exit the tunnel, Daniel heard a loud *Snap!* A whole section of the slide broke open behind him.

The slide spit him out into the landing pool. Daniel sputtered for air. He pushed his hair out of his eyes and looked back. There was a huge, gaping hole in the slide. Water poured out of it and smacked against the concrete pool deck.

Then Daniel realized something horrible. The people on the platform at the top of the slide wouldn't be able to see the hole. They wouldn't hear the kids screaming. They wouldn't know anything was wrong.

And it was Aaron's turn next.

As Aaron waited, the signal light at the top of the platform turned green.

CHAPTER 14
NO ACCIDENT

Daniel looked up at Janie. She was standing up in her lifeguard chair, looking nervously at the top of the slide. She looked ready to do something, but she wasn't yelling or signaling anyone.

"Stop the slide!" Daniel yelled, as loud as he could. "Press the red button!"

Janie did nothing. At the top of the slide, Aaron sat down to begin his run.

"Janie!" Daniel screamed. "Do something!"

Janie didn't move. She just stared at the gaping hole in the slide.

Suddenly, all around the park, the flow of water stopped. Daniel took a deep breath. Someone had shut off the water.

Then Daniel realized something. The part of the slide with the hole was the place where they'd seen the worker the day before.

This is no accident! he thought angrily.

Aaron bolted down the steps of the slide. Daniel climbed out of the pool. People were running around everywhere.

Gabe was standing near the diving pool. He had his hand on a red lever under a sign that read, "Emergency Shut Off."

As Aaron reached the bottom of the steps, Daniel ran up to him. Dozens of frightened kids were heading for the exits.

"Nobody leaves!" Gabe yelled. "I'm calling the police."

Daniel looked at Aaron. "It was the GigaMart worker," he said. "I'm sure of it. I'm going to get my phone out of the locker room. You find Janie."

"Janie?" Aaron exclaimed. "Why?"

"Just do it," Daniel said. "Find her, and don't let her leave."

Daniel sprinted toward the locker rooms. Once he had his phone, he ran back. Gabe was standing guard at the front entrance. Daniel could hear sirens in the distance.

As he ran toward Gabe, Daniel wondered if he could really trust him.

I have to, he thought. *If he were involved, he would've let someone get hurt. He wouldn't have shut off the water.*

He ran up to Gabe. "I know who is doing this," Daniel said, panting. "I have proof. I have pictures that prove who did it."

Gabe opened the phone and looked at the pictures. Daniel watched as Gabe's face got angrier and angrier.

Then he frowned. "That's weird," Gabe said. "I didn't know that Janie's boyfriend worked for the maintenance company." He showed Daniel the picture of one of the guys working on the slide.

"That's Janie's boyfriend?" Daniel exclaimed. "That proves she's behind this."

"What do you mean?" Gabe asked. "Janie's our best lifeguard."

"She's your best lifeguard because she always knows where the accidents are going to happen before they happen," Daniel explained.

"That's a big accusation," Gabe said.

"That's why she wanted to be by the green slide today," Daniel told him. "That's why she was in the water even before the diving board broke yesterday. That's why she was always in the right place to make the other rescues. And that's why she didn't do anything when the slide broke today."

"She did do one thing," came a voice from near the building. It was Aaron. He was walking toward Gabe and Daniel, holding Janie by the arm.

Aaron went on, "She pressed the green button to signal the top of the slide that it was okay to send the next person down. She pushed it after the slide broke. I know, because I was the next person in line."

CHAPTER 15
THE WALL OF HONOR

The next morning, Daniel opened the newspaper. On the front page was a story about Berry Creek. The headline read, "Lifeguard Planned Berry Creek Sabotage."

Daniel read the article. Janie had confessed to everything. She'd been jealous of her sister. She knew that earning a few plaques on the award wall at Berry Creek would prove she was a talented lifeguard too. So she'd gotten her boyfriend to loosen some screws around the park.

That left one mystery, though. *Why did Gabe tell us that Lucy Parker called the police?* Daniel wondered.

When he and Aaron arrived at the waterpark an hour later, Daniel decided to ask Gabe.

"This is embarrassing," Gabe said, frowning. "The thing is, I saw you guys fall in Mrs. Parker's backyard. I made up the whole thing. I didn't think anyone respected me enough to listen if I didn't say the police made me do it."

"We always respected you, Gabe," Daniel said. "But I really respected you after you shut the water off when the slide broke. You saved Aaron's life."

"I owe you big time," Aaron said.

"I owe you guys my job," Gabe said. "Let's just call it even."

* * *

Two weeks later, on the last day that the waterpark was open for the summer, there was another ceremony. Daniel and Aaron stood next to the mayor as everyone in the park clapped for them.

Gabe tapped the microphone and said, "Your efforts allowed our park to fix a major problem, and to continue to stay open. I can't thank you enough."

After speeches by the mayor and the police chief, Daniel and Aaron were given their plaques. They posed for pictures and shook hands with the mayor.

Then the boys' plaques were placed on the Wall of Honor, a few feet higher than the spot where Janie's plaque had once been.

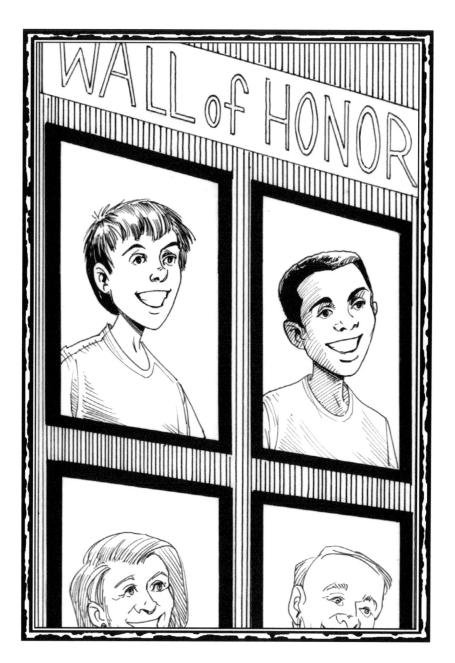

ABOUT THE AUTHOR

Bob Temple lives in Rosemount, Minnesota, with his wife and three children. He has written more than thirty books for children. Over the years, he has coached more than twenty kids' soccer, basketball, and baseball teams. He also loves visiting classrooms to talk about his writing.

ABOUT THE ILLUSTRATOR

Cynthia Martin has worked in comics and animation since 1983. Her credits include *Star Wars*, *Spider-Man,* and *Wonder Woman* for Marvel Comics and DC Comics, in addition to work as a storyboard artist for Sony Children's Entertainment and the Krislin Company. Cynthia's recent projects include an extensive series of graphic novels for Capstone Press and two issues of *Blue Beetle* for DC Comics. She also illustrated the book *Alley of Shadows,* published by Stone Arch Books.

GLOSSARY

accident (AK-si-duhnt)—something that takes place unexpectedly

binoculars (buh-NOK-yuh-lurz)—an instrument that makes distant things seem nearer

ceremony (SAIR-uh-moh-nee)—formal words spoken to mark an important occasion

complaints (kuhm-PLAYNT)—a formal charge against someone

confessed (kuhn-FESSD)—admitted to doing something wrong

lifeguard (LIFE-gard)—someone who is trained to save swimmers in danger

maintenance (MAYN-tuh-nuhnss)—a maintenance company fixes things

motives (MOH-tivz)—reasons for doing something

plaque (PLAK)—an award with words on it

sabotage (SAB-uh-tahzh)—damage of something on purpose

suspect (SUH-spekt)—someone thought to be responsible for a crime

WHAT TO DO

There are waterparks all over the world! No matter where you are or where you're traveling on vacation, you're sure to be able to find a waterpark to visit with your friends or family.

To make sure you don't have to spend all day in line, arrive early. If you get to the waterpark before noon, you'll have more time for fun!

If you go to the waterpark with a group, find a good place to use as a meeting place.

Practice smart water safety. Kids should always have adult supervision or a buddy to look out for them. Don't swim alone.

Make sure there's a lifeguard nearby before you enter the water.

AT THE WATERPARK

MAKE SURE TO BRING:

Sunscreen

Money for treats

Sunglasses

Sandals or water shoes

DON'T BRING:

Valuable things. Leave them at home!

Cell phones or other electronics that can be damaged by water

Inflatable pool toys. You'll have plenty of fun without them!

WITH THESE TIPS, YOU'LL SOON BE SPLASHING AROUND!

DISCUSSION QUESTIONS

1. Why did Janie cause the accidents at the waterpark?

2. Why did Gabe tell Aaron and Daniel that Mrs. Parker had called the police?

3. Daniel and Aaron had jobs like babysitting and mowing lawns to get money to spend at the waterpark. How do you get money to spend during the summer?

WRITING PROMPTS

1. If you had a lot of land to donate, like Mrs. Parker in this book, what would you want the land to be used for?

2. Janie was jealous of her sister. Have you ever been jealous of someone? Write about what happened.

3. Sometimes it can be interesting to think about a story from another person's point of view. Try writing chapter 2 from Janie's point of view. What does she see? What does she hear? What does she think about?

INTERNET SITES

Do you want to know more about subjects related to this book? Or are you interested in learning about other topics? Then check out FactHound, a fun, easy way to find Internet sites.

Our investigative staff has already sniffed out great sites for you!

Here's how to use FactHound:

1. Visit *www.facthound.com*

2. Select your grade level.

3. To learn more about subjects related to this book, type in the book's ISBN number: **9781434207999**.

4. Click the **Fetch It** button.

FactHound will fetch the best Internet sites for you!